Someone Fancy Is Missing

This photo album is SO boring! And no wonder—Nancy is missing from the photographs! Help add glamour to these pictures by using your stickers to put Nancy back into the scenes!

A Fabulous Entourage

(That's a fancy word meaning the people
who hang around you.)

Being fancy is a must, but it's not very fun
when no one's there to see it.
Use your stickers to fill these pages with
Nancy's very favorite people.

Tada!

It's time for Nancy to put on a breathtaking show.
Use your stickers to make sure her family and friends
are in the audience to watch!

Attention Family: Let's Get Fancy!

Nancy's family needs a little help when it comes to
looking fancy. Use your stickers to show the whole family
dressed up in their finest clothes!

X-mas ornaments

It's Not a Soiree without Dancing!
(Soiree means party in French.)

Nancy knows that having a dance floor makes any party fancier. Use your stickers to help Nancy's family and friends take a few twirls and join in the fun!

Fancy and Fun Activities with Nancy's Favorite People

Nancy knows that it's important to look your best, but you also need glamorous things to do with your precious time.
Who better to do them with than the people you love? Use your pretty stickers to decorate this page with Nancy and her family and friends doing fabulous things.

Treats to Tickle
Even the Sweetest Tooth

Nancy loves yummy foods!
If they're colorful and look fancy,
too, that's even better.
Can you use your stickers to help fill
this page with Nancy's
favorite treats?

Did Someone Say Tea Party?

Help Nancy set out all her favorite delicious treats
for a scrumptious tea party!

Oh, My!
Fancy Treats Stacked So High!

Nancy knows that delicious treats are even more fabulous when they sit on a pretty tray. Use your stickers to help Nancy pile up all her favorite treats.

Oops!

There were a few *too* many pretty treats on Nancy's tray!
Use your stickers to show the colorful array of treats
that have gone flying.

Every Girl Needs a Glamorous Abode

Nancy absolutely positively loves decorating her room! Use your stickers to help Nancy fill her room with fancy flair.

Hello, Fancy Coatrack!

Can you use your stickers to make the plain coatrack as beautiful as the fancy one? Maybe you can even make it a bit fancier!

Ooh La La!

Help Nancy get ready for a fancy spa day! Use your stickers to create a luxurious spa for Nancy.

Super duper Scooper! New!

Super duper Scooper!

New!

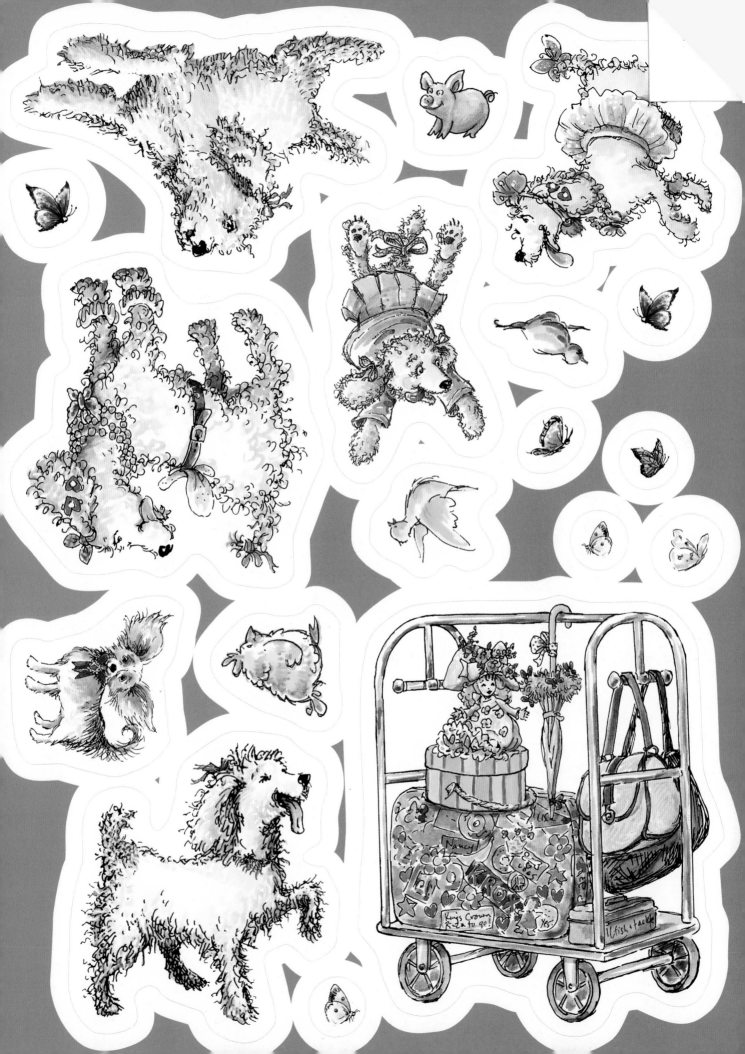

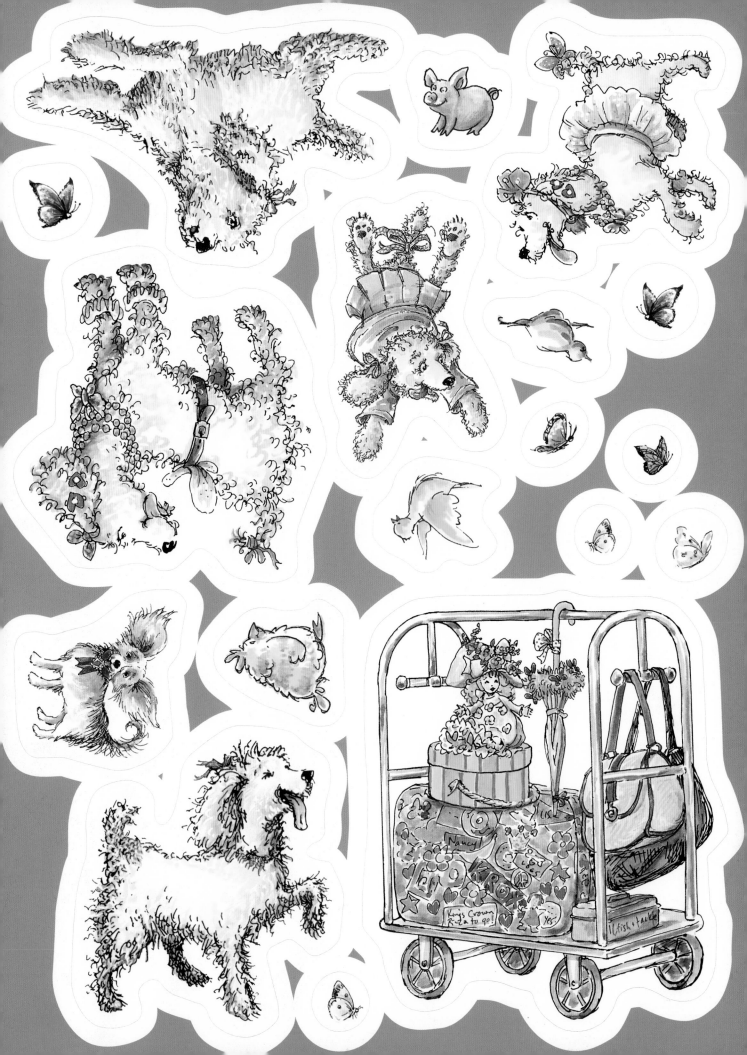

The Fabulous Faces
of Nancy

Just like having a fancy outfit for every occasion, Nancy has a face for every occasion, too! Nancy loves to make dramatic faces for each of her different moods. Fill this page with stickers of Nancy's favorite faces.

Creatures to Love! Love!! Love!!!

Nancy absolutely loves animals! Can you help fill this page with Nancy's favorite animal toys to give her a fantastic menagerie? (Menagerie is a fancy word for animal collection.)

Of course, real animals
are so much more fun!

Beautiful Butterflies

Nancy thinks butterflies are simply divine! Place your flower and butterfly stickers on these pages to create a butterfly pavilion. That's a fancy word for tent.

Frenchy Equals Fancy

Nancy's favorite animal of all is her pooch, Frenchy. Fill this page with stickers of Frenchy being fancy!